To Merry, Mabel and Joe with love   L.H.

© The Chicken House 2000

Illustrations © Lesley Harker 2000

First published in the United Kingdom in 2000 by
The Chicken House, Frome, Somerset, UK

This paperback edition published in 2001 by The Chicken House

Designed by Lisa and Ellie Sturley.
Twinkle, Twinkle Little Star was written by Jane Taylor 1783-1824
Printed and bound in Singapore

British Library Cataloguing in Publication data available.
Library of Congress Cataloguing in Publication data available.

ISBN 1 903434 18 1

Twinkle, Twinkle
Little Star

pictures by
Lesley Harker

The Chicken House

Twinkle, Twinkle, little star,

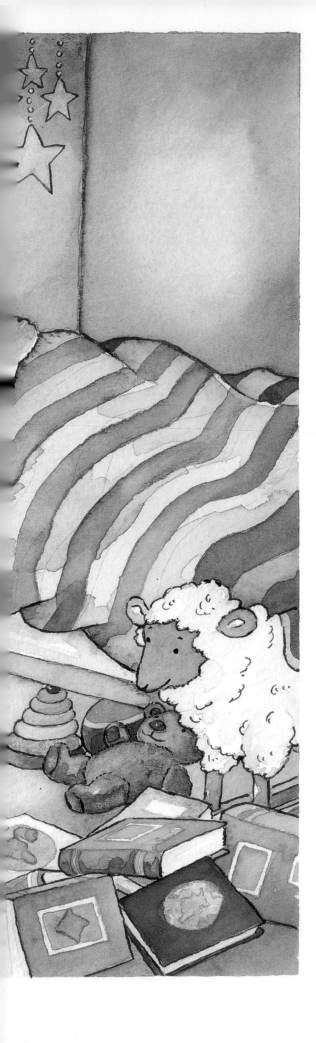

How I wonder what you are!

Up above the
world so high,
Like a diamond
in the sky.

When the blazing sun is gone,
When he nothing shines upon,
Then you show your little light,

Twinkle, Twinkle all the night.

Then the traveller in the dark,
Thanks you for your tiny spark,
He could not see which way to go,
If you did not twinkle so.

In the dark blue sky you keep,
And often through my curtains peep,
For you never shut your eye,
Till the sun is in the sky.

As your bright and tiny spark,
Lights the traveller in the dark –
Though I know not what you are,
Twinkle, Twinkle, little star.